A FEIWEL AND FRIENDS BOOK

An imprint of Macmillan Publishing Group, LLC

175 Fifth Avenue, New York, NY 10010

Printed in China by RR Donnelley Asia Printing Solutions Ltd., Dongguan City, Guangdong Province.

Our books may be purchased in bulk for promotional, educational, or business use.
Please contact your local bookseller or the Macmillan Corporate and Premium Sales Department
at (800) 221-7945 ext. 5442 or by e-mail at MacmillanSpecialMarkets@macmillan.com.

Library of Congress Cataloging-in-Publication Data is available.
ISBN 978-1-250-07635-9

Book design by Carol Ly

Feiwel and Friends logo designed by Filomena Tuosto

First edition, 2019

10 9 8 7 6 5 4 3 2 1

mackids.com

Mermaids Fast Asleep

ROBIN RIDING

illustrated by ZOE PERSICO

FEIWEL AND FRIENDS
NEW YORK

Do you suppose, way down deep,
there are mermaids fast asleep?

Wearing brightly colored scales
on their long and curvy tails.

Mermothers, merfathers too
with golden eyes and hair of blue

counting fish instead of sheep,
rocking merbabies to sleep,

while the dolphins swimming by
sing to them a lullaby:

Way down deep
Way down deep
Are there mermaids fast asleep?

If I could only swim that far
and deep to where the mermaids are.

If I could watch them lay their heads
upon their golden sandy beds,

their secret, oh, I would keep
and not disturb the mermaids' sleep.

Peaceful on the ocean floor
with now and then a gentle snore,

breathing water like it's air
way down deep, down deep, down there.

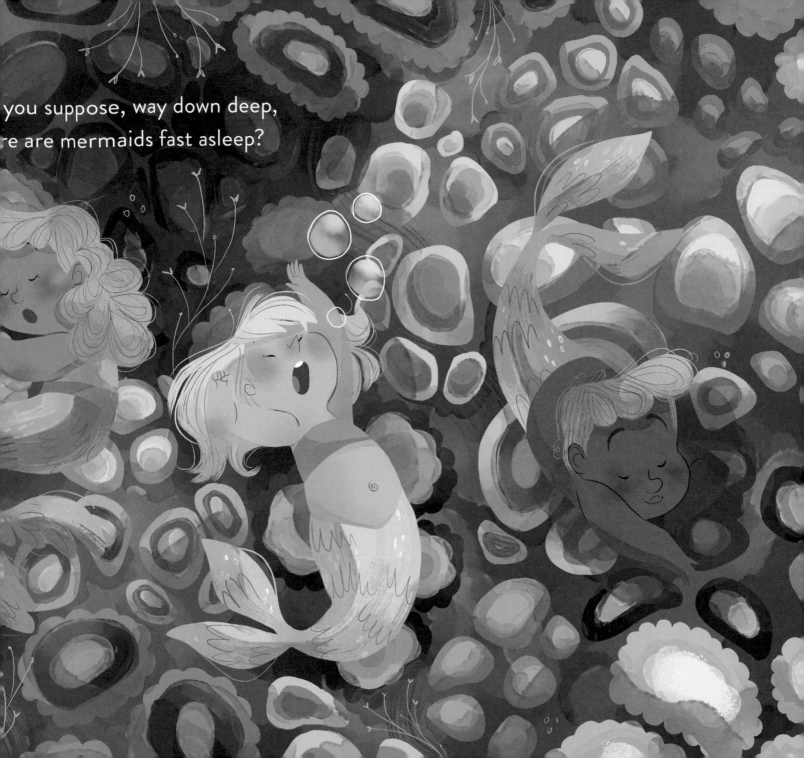

you suppose, way down deep,
re are mermaids fast asleep?

Way down deep
Way down deep
Are there mermaids fast as

Silver mermaids with golden hair
way down deep, down deep, down there?

Way down deep
Way down deep

Are there mermaids fast asleep?
Are there mermaids fast asleep?